Cuido mi salud/Keeping Healthy

Cómo cuidar mis dientes/ Taking Care of My Teeth

por/by Terri DeGezelle

Traducción/Translation: Dr. Martín Luis Guzmán Ferrer

Editor Consultor/Consulting Editor: Dra. Gail Saunders-Smith

Consultor/Consultant: Amy Grimm, MPH
Program Director, National Center for Health Education
New York, New York

Capstone press®

Mankato, Minnesota

Pebble Plus is published by Capstone Press,
151 Good Counsel Drive, P.O. Box 669, Mankato, Minnesota 56002.
www.capstonepress.com

1 2 3 4 5 6 12 11 10 09 08 07

Library of Congress Cataloging-in-Publication Data
DeGezelle, Terri, 1955–
   [Taking care of my teeth. Spanish & English]
   Cómo cuidar mis dientes = Taking care of my teeth/por/by Terri DeGezelle.
   p. cm. —(Cuido mi salud = Keeping healthy)
   Includes index.
   ISBN-13: 978-0-7368-7657-5 (hardcover)
   ISBN-10: 0-7368-7657-X (hardcover)
   1. Teeth—Care and hygiene—Juvenile literature. I. Title. II. Title: Taking care of my teeth. III. Series.
RK63.D4418 2007
617.6—dc22   2006027860

Summary: Simple text and photographs present ways to take care of your teeth—in both English
   and Spanish.

Editorial Credits
Sarah L. Schuette, editor; Katy Kudela, bilingual editor; Eida del Risco, Spanish copy editor;
   Jennifer Bergstrom, designer; Stacy Foster, photo resource coordinator

Photo Credits
Capstone Press/Karon Dubke, all

The author dedicates this book to Gabrielle and Nathaniel Willaert.

Note to Parents and Teachers

The Cuido mi salud/Keeping Healthy set supports science standards related to physical
health and life skills for personal health. This book describes and illustrates how to take
care of your teeth in both English and Spanish. The images support early readers in
understanding the text. The repetition of words and phrases helps early readers learn
new words. This book also introduces early readers to subject-specific vocabulary words,
which are defined in the Glossary section. Early readers may need assistance to read
some words and to use the Table of Contents, Glossary, Internet Sites, and Index sections
of the book.

Table of Contents

Tabla de contenidos

My Amazing Teeth

I have 20 baby teeth

in my mouth.

My baby teeth will fall out

as I grow.

Mis maravillosos dientes

Yo tengo 20 dientes de leche

en la boca. Mis dientes de leche

se caerán cuando yo crezca.

Then permanent teeth grow.
I will have 32 teeth
when I am an adult.

Después me crecerán los dientes
permanentes. Cuando sea adulto,
tendré 36 dientes.

The top part of my tooth
is the crown.
Teeth grow out of my gums.
Roots hold teeth inside
my mouth.

La parte de arriba del diente
es la corona. Los dientes crecen
en las encías. Las raíces sujetan
a los dientes en la boca.

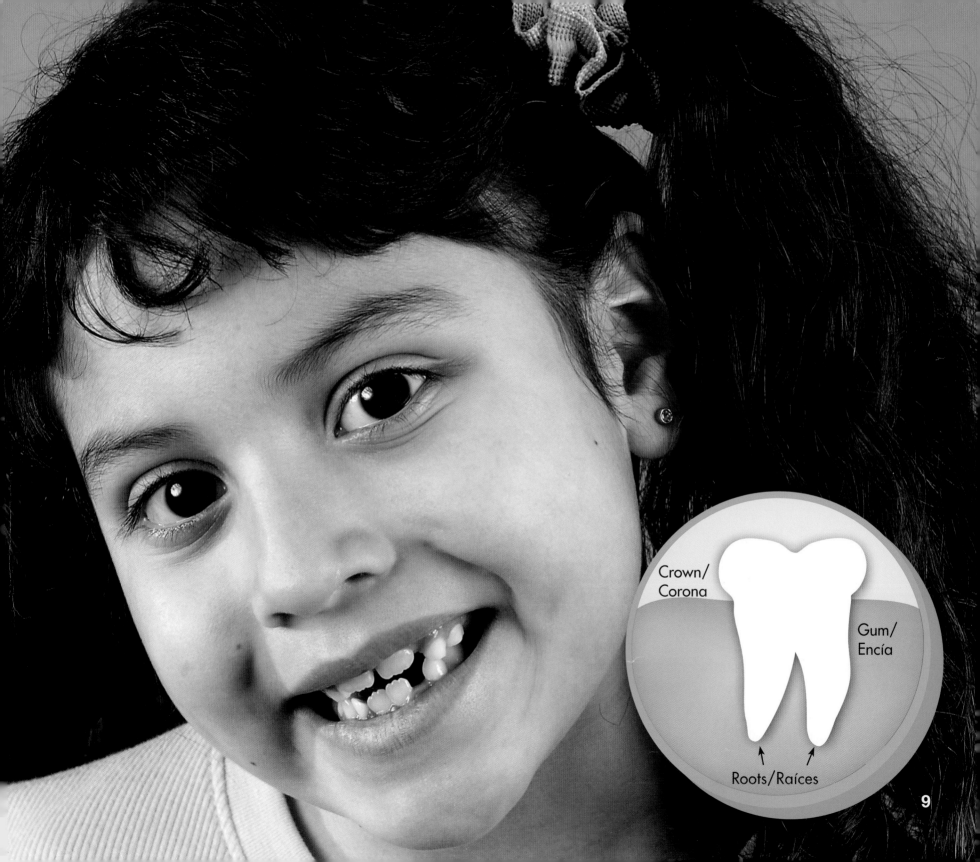

Crown/
Corona

Gum/
Encía

Roots/Raíces

9

Front teeth cut
and tear food.
Back teeth grind
and crush food.

Los dientes delanteros son para
morder y cortar la comida.
Las muelas, que están atrás, son
para masticar y triturar la comida.

The Dentist's Office

I go to the dentist's office
twice a year.
I get my teeth cleaned.

El consultorio del dentista

Yo voy al consultorio del
dentista dos veces al año.
Allí me limpian los dientes.

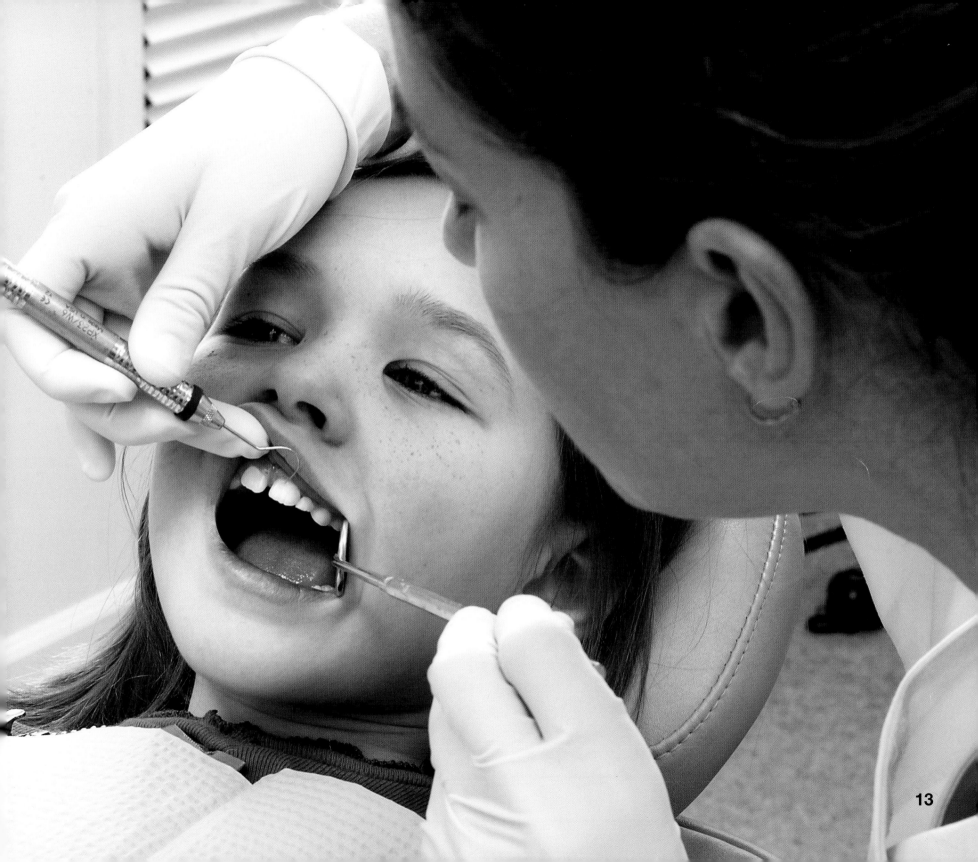

13

The dentist looks
at x-rays of my teeth.
He checks for cavities.

El dentista mira las radiografías
de mis dientes. Revisa que no
haya caries.

Healthy Teeth

I brush my teeth every day.

I brush in the morning,

after meals, and at night.

Dientes sanos

Yo me lavo los dientes todos

los días. Me los lavo por

la mañana, después de

las comidas y por la noche.

I floss between my teeth
every day.

Me los limpio todos los días
con el hilo dental.

I keep my mouth healthy
when I take care of
my teeth.

Si cuido mis dientes,
mantengo la boca sana.

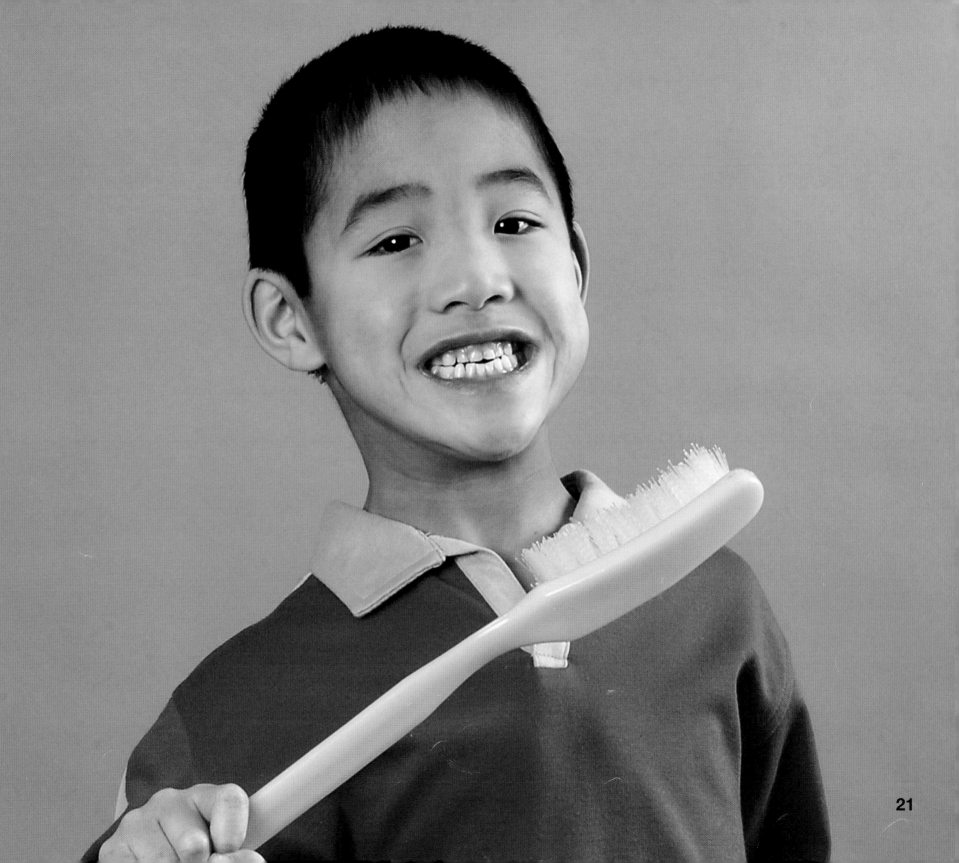

Glossary

cavity—a decayed or broken-down part of a tooth

crown—the top part of the tooth that you can see

dentist—a person who is trained to examine, clean, and fix problems with teeth

floss—to put a thin piece of dental floss between your teeth to help keep your teeth clean

gum—the firm, pink skin around the base of the tooth

root—the part of the tooth that holds it in the mouth

x-ray—a picture of the inside of a tooth

Glosario

la carie—parte picada o partida de un diente

la corona—la parte de arriba del diente que
puede verse

el dentista—la persona que estudia para examinar,
limpiar y arreglar los problemas de los dientes

la encía—la piel rosada y firme alrededor de
la base del diente

el hilo dental—un hilo muy delgado que se usa
para limpiarse entre los dientes

la radiografía—imagen de la parte interior
del diente

la raíz—la parte del diente que lo sostiene en
la boca

Internet Sites

FactHound offers a safe, fun way to find Internet sites related to this book. All of the sites on FactHound have been researched by our staff.

Here's how:

1. Visit *www.facthound.com*

2. Choose your grade level.

3. Type in this book ID **073687657X** for age-appropriate sites. You may also browse subjects by clicking on letters, or by clicking on pictures and words.

4. Click on the **Fetch It** button.

FactHound will fetch the best sites for you!

Sitios de Internet

FactHound proporciona una manera divertida y segura de encontrar sitios de Internet relacionados con este libro. Nuestro personal ha investigado todos los sitios de FactHound. Es posible que los sitios no estén en español.

Se hace así:

1. Visita *www.facthound.com*

2. Elige tu grado escolar.

3. Introduce este código especial **073687657X** para ver sitios apropiados según tu edad, o usa una palabra relacionada con este libro para hacer una búsqueda general.

4. Haz clic en el botón **Fetch It**.

¡FactHound buscará los mejores sitios para ti!

Index

Índice